This igloo book belongs to:

....

igloobooks

Published in 2022
First published in the UK by Igloo Books Ltd
An imprint of Igloo Books Ltd
Cottage Farm, NN6 0BJ, UK
Owned by Bonnier Books
Sveavägen 56, Stockholm, Sweden
www.igloobooks.com

0122 001
2 4 6 8 10 9 7 5 3 1
ISBN 978-1-80022-574-9

Written by Stephanie Moss
Illustrated by Kristen Humphrey

Designed by Hannah George
Edited by Daisy Edwards

Printed and manufactured in China

How to
REACH
the
MOON

igloobooks

Mouse wondered why
as she stared at the sky,
"I can't reach the moon.
Is it really that high?"

She **pointed** her toes...

... and she STRETCHED really tall.

But she still couldn't reach it,
for she was too small.

So, she **tiptoed** that night, in the magic moonlight,
in search of a friend who could reach the right height.

"I'll help you," said Cockerel.
"The hens all will, too.
What is it you need?
Tell us what to do."

Mouse said, "See up there?"
And they all stopped and stared.

They said, "You want us to fly all the way... where?!"

Their wings went FLAP-FLAP! How their soft feathers flew.
They spluttered and squawked, "None of us can help you!"

So, she skipped and she stepped and she finally crept
into the forest where sleepy Sloth slept.

"Can you reach the moon?" she asked. "You climb all day."
Sloth tried, but he yawned, "It's just too far away!"

Then Mouse yelled, "Yippee!" Because what did she see?
A long pair of legs, reaching tall as a tree!

Flamingo said, "Outer space does sound like fun.
But, I will show you it just can't be done."

The next plan went wrong, for although it was long...

... poor Giraffe's neck simply wasn't that strong!

Then, in the distance,
Mouse saw an old friend.
Surely her mission had
come to an end?

"Wow, what a treat that we old friends should meet."
Mouse said, "My search for this task is complete!"

So, Elephant leapt and she sprang and she soared...
But then she collapsed in a heap on the floor.

Mouse scratched her head.
"It's not over," she said.
She thought of her friends
and she sat up in bed.

'I've got a new plan,'
she wrote.

'Come to my house.
I know what to do this time.
Lots of love,
Mouse.'

A crowd soon appeared with more volunteers.
"Let's make a tower!" said Mouse, and they cheered.

At first, they all wibbled and wobbled around.

Then, with a CRASH, they fell down to the ground.

They worked side by side, and the harder they tried,
the stronger their tower grew. "Made it!" they cried.

They feasted beneath all the twinkling stars.
"With friends like you," Mouse said, "the moon's not so far!"

Moon Adventure

me and Cow

me and Sloth

yummy cupcakes!

we made it!